Hi Mom. —J.F.   Hi Mom! Hi Dad! Hi Ron! —K.S.   For Uncle Jack —J.E.D.

For information address HarperCollins Children's Books, a division of HarperCollins Publishers, 1350 Avenue of the Americas, New York, NY 10019.   www.harperchildrens.com   Library of Congress Cataloging-in-Publication Data   Fallon, Joe.   Halfway Hank / by Joe Fallon and Ken Scarborough ; illustrated by Jack E. Davis.— 1st ed.   p. cm.   Summary: Hank always does things halfway, but one day he finds a way to finish something while still being true to himself.   ISBN 0-06-623636-3 — ISBN 0-06-623637-1 (lib. bdg.)   [1. Humorous stories. 2. Stories in rhyme.] I. Scarborough, Ken. II. Davis, Jack E., ill. III. Title.   PZ8.3F215Hal 2005   2004006083   [E]—dc22   Typography by Amelia May Anderson   1 2 3 4 5 6 7 8 9 10 ❖   First Edition

Hank

By Joe Fallon
& Ken Scarborough

Illustrated by
Jack E. Davis

HarperCollins Publishers

Halfway to the edge of town,
Midway down the street,
You'll see a lawn that's just half mown
And a bike with half a seat.

That's where Hank A. Mezzomezzo
Lives in all his glory.
They call him Halfway Hank,
And this is his whole story.

Half his room was messy
And half of it was neat.
Hank always washed his face and ears
But always missed his feet.

Hank was a champ at party games
(He wore a half blindfold).
Since he counted half his birthdays,
He was really twice as old.

Hank only wore a single skate;
He said: "I don't need more."
And while his friends made figure eights,
Hank made a figure four.

His sister always said that he
Was weird as weird can be.
But Hank said, "I'm not being weird,
I'm only being me."

Hank had a halfway way of life
That no one could undo.
Until the day that fate stepped in
At the Wholenut County Hoe-Down
Days and Olde-Tyme Barbecue.

Hank joined his sister Demi's team
In spoon-and-egg–style races,
But using only half a spoon
Got egg on both their faces.

For the tracking competition
Hank brought half a map,
Which got their team completely lost.
His sister thought she'd snap.

Next they joined the rowing race
In Hank's new half canoe.
Demi warned it wouldn't float;
He found out that was true.

The square dance contest started fine.
Hank danced with lots of style.
But since he did just half the steps,
The dancers finished in a pile.

Demi wriggled, squeezed, and pushed
Till her head protruded.
"If you can't dance like us," she growled,
"Then Hank, you're not included.

You got me bruised and lost and egged
And in a dancers' knot.
You shouldn't even try at all,
If half is all you've got!"

Hank shuffled off. He sighed and said,
His voice half full of woe,
"The hundred-meter dash is next;
I know how that will go.

I'll run just half the distance,
Stopping fifty meters short.
As everybody thunders by,
My sis will laugh and snort."

"I'm not like other people,"
Said Hank with half a frown.
"I'd like to run away and find
Some halfway kind of town.

A place where semi-dances
Don't leave people in a stack.
And the finish line is always painted
Halfway down the track."

Then suddenly it hit him
Like a baseball someone threw.
Well, actually it was a ball.
An idea hit him, too.

"Giving up before the race
Is simply for the birds!"
Hank found a scrap of paper
And he wrote four little words.

When Hank approached the starting line,
His sis groaned, "Here comes trouble!
He always does things halfway,
But he'll lose this on the double!"

"On your mark," the judge announced,
"Get set . . ." He fired the gun!
It went *bang*! The runners sprang!
All, that is, but one.

While the other runners raced,
Crazily stampeding,
Hank stood at the starting line,
Coolly, calmly reading.

"What's he doing?" someone cried,
Ten yards down the track.
Demi and the others tried
To run while looking back.

Suddenly Hank blasted off
Into a whooshing run!
And in a flash he passed
The other runners one by one.

Demi wasn't worried by
Hank's speeding cheetah's pace.
She knew he'd reach the halfway point
Then stop and lose the race.

But when he reached the halfway mark,
Hank passed it like a missile!
The judge was so surprised,
He blew his nose and picked his whistle.

Hank didn't stop, Hank didn't pause
Until he broke the tape.
Hank won the hundred-meter run!
The crowd went simply ape.

Hank's sister finished second
Then got right in his face.
"How on earth could you have finished
More than half a race?"

"I did run half a race!" cried Hank.
He showed her how he'd won.
The note that Hank had written said:
"Two-hundred meter run."

Even though she'd lost to Hank,
Demi cracked half a smile,
Because he'd found a way to play
In his own halfway style.

Halfway to the edge of town,
Midway down the street,
You'll see a lawn that's just half mown
And a bike with half a seat.

Look closely, you'll see one proud sister
And one winning brother,
Half a trophy in one room,
And one half in the other.